Paddington
at the Palace

For more activities, games, books and fun, visit: www.paddington.com

First published in hardback in Great Britain by HarperCollins*Publishers* Ltd in 1986
First published in paperback by Collins Picture Lions in 2001
This edition published as part of a gift set in 2018

Collins Picture Lions is an imprint of HarperCollins*Publishers* Ltd.
HarperCollins Children's Books is a division of HarperCollins*Publishers* Ltd.

Text copyright © Michael Bond 1986
Illustrations copyright © R. W. Alley 1999

Visit our website at: www.harpercollins.co.uk

Printed in China

Michael Bond

Paddington

at the Palace

Illustrated by R. W. Alley

HarperCollins *Children's Books*

One morning Paddington and Mr Gruber set
out to see the Changing of the Guard at
Buckingham Palace.

Mr Gruber took his camera, Paddington took
a flag on a stick in case he saw the Queen,
and they both sat on the front seat of the bus
so that they could see all the places of interest
on the way.

The bus took them most of the way, then they had to walk through St James's Park.

It was a lovely sunny morning and there were flowers everywhere.

"I think I may pick some for the Queen," said Paddington.

"I'm afraid that's against the law," said Mr Gruber. "This is what is known as a Royal Park, and all the flowers belong to the Queen anyway. Besides, it would spoil it for others.

"If you like I'll take a picture for your scrapbook instead."

"Fancy having a front garden as big as this," said Paddington. "I wonder if she has to mow the lawn?"

Mr Gruber laughed and then, as they drew
near to some large gates, he pointed towards
the roof of a building behind them.

"We're in luck's way, Mr Brown," he said.
"There's a flag flying. That means the Queen
is at home."

Paddington peered through the railings and
waved his own flag several times in case the
Queen was watching.

"I think I saw someone at one of the
windows, Mr Gruber," he called excitedly.
"Do you think it was the Queen?"

"Who knows?" said Mr Gruber.

Soon afterwards they heard the sound of a band playing. The music got louder and louder and there was a lot of shouting and the *clump*, *clump* of marching feet.

But by then there were so many people,
Paddington couldn't see a thing.

Mr Gruber wondered whether he ought to suggest holding Paddington up to see, but in the end he bought him a periscope instead.

"If you look through the bottom end," he explained, "you can see over the top of people's heads."

Paddington tried it out, but all he could see were other people's faces and he didn't think much of some of those.

In the end he tried crawling through the legs of the crowd, but by the time he got to the other side the band had passed by.

"Look," said a small boy, pointing at Paddington. "One of the soldiers has dropped his hat."

"It's what they call a busby, dear," said his mother.

Paddington jumped to his feet. "I'm not a *busby*," he cried. "I'm a bear!"

Gradually the crowd melted away until there were only a few people left.

"Oh dear," said Mr Gruber. "It's all over and I didn't even get a picture of you with one of the guardsmen."

"I didn't even *see* them," said Paddington sadly.

Just then a man in a bowler hat said
something to a policeman by the gate,
and then pointed towards Paddington
and Mr Gruber.

The policeman beckoned to them. "I've instructions to invite you inside so that you can take a proper photograph," he called. "You're very honoured."

Paddington felt most important as he and
Mr Gruber followed the policeman across
the Palace parade ground and the guard
came to attention.

"I think," he said, as he stood to attention while Mr Gruber took a photograph, "this guard is so good he doesn't need changing."

As they left the Palace, Paddington stopped by the gates to wave his flag.

"Do you think it was the Queen looking out of the window when we first came?" he asked.

"It was either the Queen," said Mr Gruber, "or it was someone who likes bears very much."

And he took one last picture for Paddington's scrapbook. "You must mark the window with a cross when you paste it in — just in case."

Me at the Palace.

Look out for more fantastic books about
Paddington